The Bay School BLOGGER

by Nan Walker
illustrated by Amy Wummer

Kane Press
New York

Library of Congress Cataloging-in-Publication Data

Walker, Nan.
  The Bay School blogger / by Nan Walker ; illustrated by Amy Wummer.
     p. cm. — (Social studies connects)
  "History & Culture/The Spread of Ideas-Grades: 1/3."
  Summary: When Bailey starts a blog about her school, her hardest task is keeping her identity a
secret, especially when her ideas for fixing the problem of overly-heavy backpacks make her blog
famous.
  ISBN: 978-1-57565-258-0 (alk. paper)
  [1. Blogs—Fiction. 2. Schools—Fiction. 3. Identity—Fiction.] I. Wummer, Amy, ill. II. Title.
  PZ7.W153643Bay 2008
  [E]—dc22
                                    2007026566

eISBN 978-1-57565-671-7

10 9 8 7 6 5 4 3 2

First published in the United States of America in 2008 by Kane Press, Inc.
Printed in China.

Social Studies Connects is a trademark of Kane Press, Inc.

Book Design: Edward Miller

Visit us online at **www.kanepress.com**

  Like us on Facebook
facebook.com/kanepress

Follow us on Twitter
@kanepress

I dump my two-ton backpack on the floor. *Thud!* "Why can't our books be on CDs?" I moan. "Then they wouldn't be so heavy."

"Great idea!" My friend Joel fakes a toss. "And we could use them to play Frisbee, too!"

"Can you guys pipe down?" my sister April says. "I'm reading Ruler of the World."

April loves that blog. She reads it every day.

"Our teacher should have a blog," I tell Joel. "Writing homework on the board is so old-timey."

Joel says, "Maybe *you* should start a blog, Bailey. You've got lots of cool ideas." He grins. "You could call it Ruler of the School."

RULER OF THE WORLD
If I ruled the world, books would be waterproof so you could read in the shower.

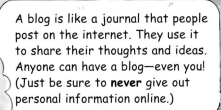

A blog is like a journal that people post on the internet. They use it to share their thoughts and ideas. Anyone can have a blog—even you! (Just be sure to **never** give out personal information online.)

Hmm. That might be fun. I picture kids reading my blog, talking about it, pointing at me. . . . *Yikes!* "No way," I say. "Too much attention!"

Joel snaps his fingers. "I've got it! You could be like Spiderman."

I stare at him. "Climb walls? Spin webs?"

"Secret identity," he says. "No one has to know that Bailey Lewis is the Ruler of the School."

The more I think about it, the less crazy it
seems. Why not write a blog? I have a zillion ideas.
What if we took a field trip to a donut factory?
What if we learned circus tricks in gym?
What if we had paintball on the playground?
Okay, maybe that's not such a great idea.

April helps me set up my blog. It looks really awesome. Readers can even write in by clicking on "Backtalk."

I can't wait to hear what everyone says on Monday!

Can You Imagine?
Before writing was invented, people mostly shared ideas by talking. If a person lived far away, you had to send a messenger. That could take a long time. And sometimes the messages got mixed up!

RULER OF THE SCHOOL

BACK TALK!

On the way to school I listen hard, but
no one mentions Ruler of the School.

No one is talking about it in the hallway, either.

Or in class.

"I can't believe it," I complain to Joel. "I worked on that blog all weekend!"

He looks at me. "Does anyone know about it?"

Oh. "Guess I need to get the word out. But how can I do that without spilling my secret identity?"

"Don't worry," Joel says. "I have a plan."

COMPUTER LAB

Can You Imagine?

Long ago people came up with clever ways to send simple messages over several miles. Some people tapped out messages on drums. Others sent up puffs of smoke from special fires!

9

Joel and I hang back when computer lab is over.
We move quickly from computer to computer.
When the next class comes in, Ruler of the School
will be on every screen.

And best of all, no one knows it's ME!

About 5,000 years ago, writing
started to appear. It totally
changed the way people
shared news and ideas.

As soon as I get home, I switch on the computer. Joel's plan worked! Somebody read my blog and left a message!

Bob? . . . Who is Bob?

BACK TALK!

Donut factory? How about a field trip to outer space? Blast off! Jupiter, here we come!

Backtalk Bob

Can You Imagine?
Writing helped spread ideas, but it didn't solve every problem. A few hundred years ago, a letter could take months to get across the ocean. And sometimes it never got across at all!

The next day I hear a boy ask his friend, "Have you seen Ruler of the School?"

"No, what's that? A new movie?"

"A new blog," he says, "about Bay School!"

"Cool—who's the blogger?"

The boy lowers his voice. "No one knows."

I sneak a look. Could *he* be Bob?

So, how do good ideas catch on? One way is by "word-of-mouth." One person tells an idea to another person. That person tells a third person—and so on!

Soon everyone is reading my blog.

I say we should replace those boring hallway posters with spray-paint art. The art club kids love that.

The cheerleaders love my idea to change our mascot from a bulldog to a basset hound. Much cuter!

I get messages from kids at other schools, too. One boy even writes in from Australia!

But no matter what ideas I come up with, I always hear from Backtalk Bob.

I say the cafeteria should buy milk from nearby farms. Bob says we should just get our own cow.

I say the school should order comic books for the library. Bob says we should turn the library into a giant moon bounce.

"Who is Ruler of the School, anyway?" I complain. "Him or me?"

Joel laughs. "I think Backtalk Bob is funny."

"Silly is more like it. None of his ideas are for real, like mine. At least mine *could* be real. . . ."

That gets me thinking. "I wonder how I could make something really big happen," I say.

"How about making tomorrow Backwards Day?" Joel says. "You know, everyone wears their clothes backwards, walks backwards, talks backwards. . . ."

"How do you *talk* backwards?" I ask.

He shrugs. "Wonk t'nod I."

How can you make something big happen? Start small. When 13-year-old Chester Greenfield went ice skating in 1873, his ears got cold. So he came up with an idea: earmuffs. His little idea was a big success!

The best ideas often make people's lives better. If you think of a good way to fix a problem, your idea will probably catch on!

We drop our bags and take a rest.
Backwards Day would be okay, I guess.
But I want to do something important.
Something all the kids would care about.

"I know!" I tell Joel. "Heavy backpacks—they bug everybody. But what can we do?"

"A massage chair at every desk?"

I roll my eyes. "Now you sound like Bob."

April is no help either. "Wait till middle school. Our packs are twice as heavy."

"They are not!" I say.

"Are too!"

We head for the bathroom scale.

Hey, that's it! What if all the kids put signs on their backpacks saying how much they weigh? How cool would that be? I sit down at the computer. Ruler of the School will ask everybody to do it—tomorrow!

But in the morning when I rush to the
computer, the only message is from Backtalk Bob.

How come no one said anything about my
idea? Did they all think it was dumb?
    If I'm the only one with a sign, I'll look weird.
And my secret identity might be revealed!
    I unzip my pack and stuff the sign inside.

As soon as I get to school, I see the signs. They're everywhere!

"I hear we're getting lockers!" a boy says.

"I hear we're getting two books for each class—one for school, and one to keep at home."

"I hear they found a real flying backpack on a UFO that crashed out in the desert."

A fifth-grade girl glances at me and whispers something to her friend. My stomach does a flip. Have they figured out my secret identity?

Then the girl asks me, "Where's your sign? Didn't you read Ruler of the School?"

Whew! That was close.

Thomas Jefferson was one of the people who thought America should become its own country. Great ideas can inspire millions of people to make something really big happen!

July 4, 1776

Just as everyone finally settles down for class, the loudspeaker squawks, *"Would the writer of the Ruler of the School blog please report to the main office?"*

I freeze.

Behind me, someone murmurs, "Oooh . . . trouble!"

Can You Imagine?
Even brilliant ideas can run into trouble. Alexander Graham Bell tried to sell his idea for the first telephone to a big company. They told him his phone was just a toy!

The speaker blasts again. It's louder this time.
"Please report to the main office . . . NOW."

I look at Joel. He looks at me.

I stand up very slowly. My legs wobble like
Jell-O. I can feel all the kids staring at me. My ears
burn as the whispers fill the room.

It's Bailey! Bailey is the Ruler of the School!

Joel stands up. "I told you to write the blog, Bailey. I'll go with you."

Before I can say anything, someone yells, "Me too—I'll come along! I love Ruler of the School!"

"Me three!"

"We should all go!"

"Bailey! Bailey! Ruler of the School!"

In the end, only Joel gets to come along.

"So, Bailey," the principal says, staring down at me. "You're the mystery blogger."

I gulp and nod.

Suddenly she breaks into a smile. "Nice work!"

Guess what? The principal wants me to talk to the school board about the backpack problem.

Plus, she is a big fan of my blog!

"Especially Backtalk Bob," she says, and laughs. "A moon bounce in the library—I love it!"

Joel smiles. "Thanks!"

I stare at him. *Joel?* Joel is Backtalk Bob?

He looks at me and grins. "Hey, I wanted a cool secret identity, too!"

All I can do is laugh.

Six weeks later I sling my light-as-air backpack over my shoulder. "I can't believe the school board gave us lockers."

"Thanks to your blog," Joel says. "So what's next for Ruler of the School?"

"I think I'll take a break for a while," I say.

"Don't tell me you ran out of ideas!"

I smile. "Nope . . ."

IDEAS ON THE MOVE!

Talking   Writing   Printing Press

"I'm just too busy reading everybody else's blogs!"

THEN AND NOW!

WHAT'S
NEXT
??

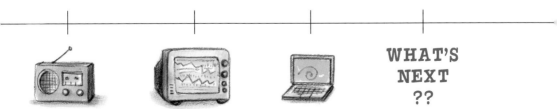

We can express ideas!

MAKING CONNECTIONS

Bailey's ideas could change the world! Well, they can at least change her *school*. Your ideas can make a difference, too. But it's your job to **express** them. That means telling others about your ideas—by talking, or writing, or any way you choose!

Look Back

- Look at pages 6–7. What are some of Bailey's cool ideas? How does she decide to express them to others? How would you choose to share your ideas?
- On page 7, how can others express what they think about Bailey's ideas? Do you like hearing what people think of *your* ideas?
- Bailey wants to make a difference. What idea does she come up with? How does she share her idea on page 20? Does it work? Why do you think so?

Try This!

Suppose your school had its very own secret blogger! Write a story about the ideas the blogger would come up with. Would they make a difference?

Don't forget to share your story with others. That's how ideas spread!

The Ruler of MY School

Remember—Safety First!

The internet is totally amazing but it can be dangerous, too. Never, ever give out your name or other information. And no matter what you do, always get an adult's permission first!